NOAH
AND THE
ANIMALS

NOAH
AND THE
ANIMALS

For Lucy

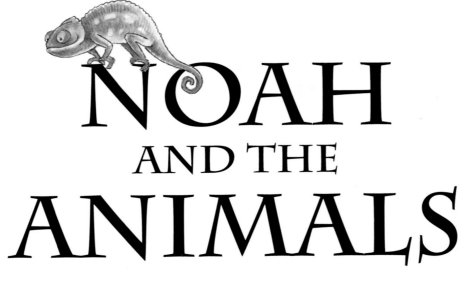

NOAH
AND THE
ANIMALS

PRUE THEOBALDS

Blackie Children's Books

Once, long ago, the world was beautiful, but wicked people began to spoil it. When God saw this He was angry.

In all the world there was only one good person left, an old, old man called Noah.

God said to Noah, 'I will make a great flood to cover all the earth and wash the wickedness away, but you and your family will be saved. You must build an ark. Build it high and wide, with windows all around and a great door in the side.'

When Noah had built the ark, God sent him out to find two of every living creature, one male and one female, and take them into the ark.

Noah went out and called to the animals, the huge elephants, the hippos and the jumping kangaroos.

He went out onto the plains and found the lions,
the tigers and all the fast running animals.

He searched out all the rats and the mice and the small, scurrying creatures of the forest.

Noah looked up at the sky and called down all the birds, the great eagles and the tiny wrens.

He searched warily for the crocodiles, the lizards, the snakes and all the scaly creatures that crawl along the ground.

Then he peered amongst the grass and under stones, looking for the small, creeping, crawling things, the slugs and snails and wriggling worms.

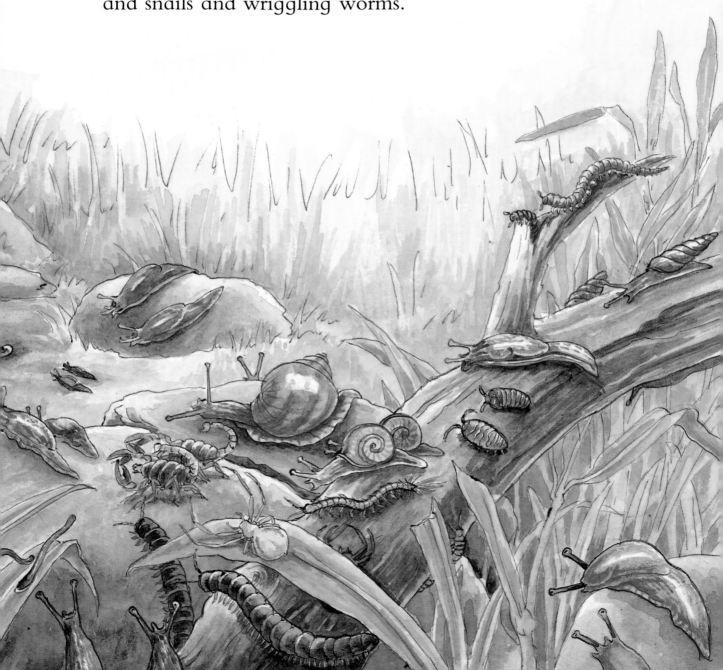

Noah called to all the insects, the butterflies, the shiny beetles, the chirping grasshoppers and the hurrying ants.

When all the animals were safely inside the ark and the door was shut, the rain came. It rained and rained as it had never rained before. Soon the ark was floating, and from the windows Noah and the animals could only see the tops of the trees.

It rained for days and nights until there was no more land to see, only the ark tossing on a huge, stormy ocean.

After many, many months the rain stopped and slowly the water began to go down.

Then one day Noah saw that the ark had come to rest on the top of a mountain. He waited until all the water had dried up and he could see trees and green grass again.

Then Noah opened the door of the ark and brought all the animals out into the new, fresh green land.

God was glad to see Noah and all the animals come safely out of the ark. He promised that never again would He bring a flood that would cover the whole world. Then He spread a great rainbow across the sky. 'This is my promise to you,' He said. 'Whenever you see the rainbow, remember, and rejoice in the wonderful world I have given you.'

BLACKIE CHILDREN'S BOOKS

Published by the Penguin Group
Penguin Books Ltd. 27 Wrights Lane, London W8 5TZ England
Penguin Books USA Inc., 375 Hudson Street, New York, New York 10014, USA
Penguin Books Australia Ltd. Ringwood, Victoria, Australia
Penguin Books Canada Ltd. 10 Alcorn Avenue, Toronto, Ontario, Canada M4V 3B2
Penguin Books (NZ) Ltd. 182-190 Wairau Road, Auckland 10, New Zealand

Penguin Books Ltd. Registered Offices: Harmondsworth, Middlesex, England

First published 1993
3 5 7 9 10 8 6 4 2

Text and illustrations copyright © Prue Theobalds, 1993

The moral right of the author and illustrator has been asserted

A CIP catalogue record for this book is available from the British Library

ISBN 0216 94002 8 (Hbk)
ISBN 0216 94003 6 (Pbk)

Printed in Hong Kong